# Aurelia's Diary 8;

## A Nice Little Bow

By. Benjamin N. Thurber

*Forward*

When I started my other series of stories, I never really was quite satisfied with their endings.  It is kind of surreal, to me, at this point, that I finally found a series where I believe the ending is just as I would want it.

Yes, Aurelia's story is going to wrap in this book, and quite a ride it's been.  I mean, ever since I conceived of creating a daughter that would grow from girl to woman in a series of books, I found a friend and former narrator in Talon David, the one who, I believe, best brought Aurelia to life with her talented voice.  She's so worth the listen, she's that good.  But, if you've been listening to the audiobooks, by this point, you already know that Talon couldn't finish the series and have welcomed Chelsea Napier into the fold.

I've also fallen in love, which is honestly something I never thought would happen again.  She is so worth it though.

But what about Aurelia?  I mean, over the past year since I started writing it, she really has grown from a girl with a marvelous attitude into a woman, ready to take on things on her own.  We'll get to finally answer the question if she'll ever give her heart to someone.

Thanks to everyone who made this series possible.  Thanks to all my friends on Facebook who supported this crazy idea of wanting to see what sort of daughter I might have had with Amanda before she passed away.  Thanks to Katrina, who helped out more than she remembers.  Thanks to all the real people and real products and places that helped, although I'm still not sponsored by any of them.

And thanks to you guys for sticking with the ravings of a madman who wanted to see what kind of daughter he might have raised.

Now let's wrap it up.

August 20, 2027

I mean, okay, I'm kind of glad to be out of there. Dad and Martha have been so *in love* since they got back from their honeymoon it's kind of been disgusting. Okay, not disgusting, romantic. I mean, they're obviously very much in love, but I think that the decision Molly and I made would go a long ways towards helping that out.

I accepted the job of being one of the English teachers at Ogden High. I've been a bulldog, a bronco, a razorback, but now, I'm a tiger.

We had a family road trip here, just like before. Dad and Martha wanted to make sure we got all settled into our new place. I mean, it's not much, but it's ours.

I guess I should say that Molly accepted the offer to be my roommate. I guess she's not too embarrassed having her older sister be one of the teachers at her new school. So, we have this little two-bedroom apartment. It's not much, but it's home. And we have a car that we can take to school.

Molly is looking for her own car and a job so she can help out. She's such a good little sister that, sometimes, I forget we're not even related by blood.

We've spent some time going through the town. It's not a bad place, with our own temple and everything, and the church is so strong here. Yes, we're in Utah, and it's obvious that the church is strong here. We can't go more than 10 miles outside the city without running into another church building.

Here I thought that Boise was strong with the church, with the institute and everything and having so many students packed into the whole area. No, it's not as strong as it is here. But, at the same time, I can't help but wonder.

I mean, yeah, I know that the world has lower standards, but I thought that coming to Utah would have a difference. Here, in Fred Meyer's, there are still a lot of outfits that show that the standards aren't universal. Plenty of belly-baring tops and tops that frankly show too much skin.

And they're worn, too. It's like there are those, here, who don't really understand the standards set up or they just don't care.

But I shouldn't be too harsh.  It's not like the whole state belongs to the church.  I'm sure there are plenty who still see our standards and wonder if they're constricting.

But I still have to smile.  I mean, I've seen Dad treat Martha with such kindness and consideration.  It was such a marvelous thing to behold, the way Martha always seemed to smile.  She is his lady, and he loves her unconditionally.  He's such a gentleman to her.

Molly said it's just the way her real dad treated her mom too.  Maybe that's another reason they are so attracted to each other.

And who knows, Molly and I may just have a younger sibling sooner or later.


August 23, 2027

Today was the day.  Today was my first real day as a teacher, and it was something to be remembered.  I mean, I have my ideas on it, and I was told by my fellow teachers not to get too attached or anything.  Some of them wanted to give me pointers, which I took in kind.

But that wasn't why I became a teacher.  No, it was something like what happened today.

I mean, sure, I've been in classrooms where the teachers decorated according to their tastes.  I've been in English Lit rooms where the teacher posts a picture or a bust of Shakespeare, and I might get to him later, but I didn't want that.  As I got ready, Molly told me she was going to ride the bus, she gave me a thumbs up.  I wanted to appear nice, but not like I was going to be the boss over my classroom.

As I sat, waiting for the first bell, I prayed.  I had to, knowing that there would be about 100-200 strangers invading my space, but it wasn't my space, not really.  I was just their guardian, temporarily.

And then the first of my students walked in, a pretty girl, about 16 or 17.  I smiled at her, and she asked if I knew when the teacher would get here.  I had to laugh when I told her I already was.  She seemed surprised, but glad that I wasn't some overbearing monarch of the classroom.

As I had already prepared for the entire week, I stood, once they all got in, and started with just one question.  Name a book that has been turned into a movie.  It doesn't have to be a recent book, but it has to have been turned into a movie.

That first girl, Chelsea, raised her hand and I called on her by name.  That surprised everyone as she said, "Pride and Prejudice."

I commended her on her choice.  A lot of Jane Austin's books have been turned into movies, and for the same reason.  She had a theme that ran though her stories, one that resonates even today.

It was the same with all the classes, they mentioned a book that had been turned into a movie that inevitably led to the same theme.

So, I kind of started pontificating on it.  I mean, yeah, it keeps going through literature, the idea that one might think themselves better than another, whether it be by money, by blood or even, in the case of Harry Potter, which was mentioned in the 5th hour, by having an all-natural attachment to something.

And I pointed out, in each instance, how many societies started to divide into classes based on these things.  Somewhere along the line, someone with a lot of money decides that they, and they alone, have the right to decide things for everyone else.  It's like they believe that they're better than the others in "lower classes."

I mentioned a few more examples where this was the case, like Hunger Games.  Those who were in the upper classes decided to pit those of the lower classes against each other for some kind of reward, and the more brutal the contest, the more the upper classes were entertained.

But is that really the case?  I mean, in actuality, don't those who have a lot of money really owe that fact to others?  How many farmers feed those who call themselves "upper class?"  I asked that, and there were a few who nodded in agreement.  Yet farmers aren't called "upper class."  Why?

What is the actual difference between the farmer and the person they feed who's considered "upper class?"  In reality, it's one thing and one thing only, money.  And those with the money inevitably start to think that they have the right to decide for the rest of us, whether we agree or not.

It's not a fair system, that way, nor is it fair to take advantage of those who don't have a lot of money by promising something that won't happen, namely that those they put in power will "redistribute" the money to them. That's never happened, not really.

No, the only way a real fair system can happen is if those with the money remember that those without are still human beings. One person is no better than the other. Sure, I'm a teacher, but that only means I want to impart the knowledge I have to my students, not that I'm somehow better than they are.

When we remember that the differences we perceive as being between us really don't exist, we see each other as we truly are. We don't see skin color, wealth or even religious affiliation as a defining trait, we see them as something that only tells the story of an individual who is not unlike us in any meaningful content.

For their assignment, I gave them all something easy. It was my first homework assigning, so I wanted it to be easy for everyone.  Download the Kindle app if they didn't already have it and get the public domain book *Frankenstein*.

I'm going to have some fun with my students.


September 6, 2027

I didn't know if we should celebrate Mom's birthday last Friday or not, given that I have a stepmom now.  When I asked Dad, he said it was just fine, as did Martha.  So, Molly and I celebrated.

And Molly got up in Fast and Testimony meeting yesterday, telling how grateful she was, to Heavenly Father, that she now has a full family, including a new big sister that she thinks is amazing.  Of course, she's quite the charmer in the Young Women's group of our new ward, which basically makes up our entire apartment building.  But she's going to be in Relief Society with me at the beginning of the year.  I wonder how that'll transition for her.

But, today, I had to hand back my students' first assignment.  For the past two weeks, they've been reading Mary Shelley's *Frankenstein*, and I wanted them to give me their ideas and feelings on it, besides giving me a rundown of the story.  I also told them I'd be able to tell who really read the book and who just thought they could watch the movie and get away with it.

Yes, some did.  More than a few, and they got lower grades. I hated to do it, but I even had to give out two F's because it was obvious that they weren't even really trying.  I mean, I know that some teachers claim we should mollycoddle the students, but I want them to really put in the effort in order to understand the lesson.

There was one that really did deserve the A she got, one that pointed something out that I really had to applaud.

And I kind of made a point of this student's pointing it out, although I didn't call her by name, to all my classes today.

The observation was that the creature in Frankenstein wasn't the real monster, Victor Frankenstein was.  I had to expand on that idea.

And it's true.  I told all my classes this, that, in the story, Victor, who wanted to play God, and play with life and death over the early losses he suffered, created something he found repulsive and summarily rejected him.  But what did the creature do?  He wasn't the lumbering zombie-like brute from the original

Frankenstein movie, not at all.  He found somewhere to live, found out about collecting rainwater and making fire.

And then he found himself getting attached to a family that he could observe and learn from.  He learned to speak, learned to read, all on his own, but he had one basic desire.

He desired to be accepted, to belong somewhere.  He desired companionship.

When the family that he'd grown so attached to summarily rejected him because he looked repulsive, he came to his creator, asking for him to create a companion for him.

When he didn't the creature turned on Frankenstein's family, starting to kill everyone in it, including his new bride.  Frankenstein was driven mad by this and desired to destroy the very thing he created.

But I decided that I'd point something out, something that would have changed the story entirely.  What if Victor hadn't rejected what he'd created?  What if that family had taken the creature in, maybe even given him a name?

What would've happened had Victor decided to take pity on the creature when he made his request and made a companion for him?

Is it really such a remarkable thing to realize that, had Victor decided to take responsibility for what he'd made?  What if, like the god he wanted to be, he had compassion for what he'd created?

What if, instead of fleeing, Victor decided to take the creature under his wing and teach it about life and about happiness?  What if, instead of having his wife killed on his wedding night, he introduced the creature to his wife, and she unquestionably loved him?

How many times do we see someone who does something that they don't take responsibility for?  How many people in my classroom, and I included myself, have done that, refused to take responsibility?

How many times do we see something or someone we find disturbing or horrible or disgusting and decide we don't want to have anything to do with them?  Sure, we talked about the character of Igor from the movies, but what was his role?  He was disfigured, and he was subservient because of it.  What would've happened had

Victor decided to make him, instead of a servant, a partner?

And what would happen if we made the same choice?

Instead of deciding that someone isn't worth it because of their

looks or because they have some kind of mental disorder, we sat

with them and got to know them?

I'm not sure I got through to everyone, but, for me, that was

a very important lesson to teach.

Actually, I did get through to someone.  I just got an

anonymous email from someone, not sure who, but they told me that

they'd been considering killing themselves because they never felt

accepted.  I changed their minds.

I saved their life.


September 10, 2027

Okay, I haven't been a big sister for very long, but I know I

love Molly.  She loves the fact that we always pray together every

morning and evening, and that I insist we pray before we eat.  I'm still working on becoming a good cook, but I'm getting there.  And she loves the fact that we read scripture together.

I mean, yeah, she's in her Senior year of high school, the very same one I teach at, but she's not in any of my classes as per school policy.  We've had plenty of laughs, plenty of board games, I still have to play her easy at checkers, and plenty of time when we just sit together watching some corny movie.

Of course, she knows to leave me alone when I have to prepare for class the next day.  But it's the weekend.  And I gave my students an assignment to be able to read whatever they want and prepare a very good presentation as a book report.  That's due after General Conference, so I expect I'll have some time to get other things prepared.

But then, as I came home, she looked so frustrated.  I had to ask what was wrong, and she told me.

Yeah, she's been on a couple of dates since we got here.  Girl's a real chip off the old block.  But she told me about this one guy who simply won't take no for an answer.  He keeps asking her to go with him, but she keeps saying no.

I asked if he was good looking, but she just scoffed and told me that wasn't what was important to her.  No, he gave of this creepy vibe, like he thought he was God's gift to women, but it wasn't God.  It was the other guy.

I asked for his name but didn't recognize it.  He's not in any of my classes, and I'm still learning all their names.  They're kind of surprised when I can call them by name, which is a good thing.

I mean, all I could do was offer some ice cream, which we shared, feeling better as we ate.  I don't know what she'll do, but she's a strong girl, raised by a strong woman.

And she's my sister.


September 21, 2027

Man, I cannot believe how I feel tonight.  I'm still mad, but I'm not seeing red anymore, just for a little bit earlier today.  And then I'm feeling a little pumped as well.

You see, that jerk that wouldn't take no for an answer from Molly, apparently, snapped.  Here I was, just walking down the hall, when I heard my little sister's voice yelling at someone, then screaming.  There was a crowd gathering already when I pushed my way through.

He'd grabbed her arm, dragging her away, telling her that he was going to show her how a man should treat a woman.  No, that is NEVER how a man should treat a woman, not EVER.  I had to step in, not only as a schoolteacher, but also as a big sister.

I asked him if he really thought that, asking him what he intended to do with Molly.  He snarled at me, telling me to keep my nose out of it, but I had to maintain control.

I saw a few phones but didn't really pay attention to them as I stated that he knew I couldn't.  He asked what business it was of mine, so I told him that, as a teacher, I had to report this, and his clear violation of the law.  As a big sister, I was willing to kick his butt over what he was intending to do with Molly.

He laughed.  I mean, sure, he's a few inches taller than I am, and muscular, but that was nothing.  He had to challenge me and ask me if I really thought I could take him.

I calmly informed him that, while I was on my mission, I took down 3 guys, bigger than he was, without a scratch.  I mean, it was kind of a lie, but I wanted him to get the point.  I told him that, if he did attack me, he'd be liable and arrested, but I wouldn't be held responsible as I would be defending myself and Molly.  I heard a number of people consent to the fact that I'd be defending, not attacking.

The guy dropped Molly's arm after a minute of consideration, snarling at her that she wasn't worth his time.  Molly collapsed in the corner, shaking, so I had to gather her in my arms, just holding onto her.

I told her that he'd never bother her again, especially if she wanted to press charges.  We'd get a restraining order if she wanted.  That would teach him a lesson.

I took her to the office, reporting the whole incident.  A few of the students came in with their phones, showing their videos as proof of what I did.  They called me a real hero, then one of the girls asked if what I said was true.  Did I really take down 3 big guys without a scratch?

I had to admit I did fudge it a little.  They came at me one at a time and I did suffer some broken ribs, but, yeah, they were arrested.

The principal seemed interested.  She wondered if I'd be willing to teach a little bit of Brazilian Jiu Jitsu, when I clarified what it was, I was trained in, as an extracurricular class.  I said I'd be interested, and she said that she'd have to clear it with the board.

Molly's okay tonight.  She called Martha and Dad, telling them I was the hero of the day.  I don't know about it, but I had to smile at the compliment.

And something tells me this class is going to be very interesting.


September 26, 2027

I'm not sure how I feel about today.  I mean, yes, it's Mom and Dad's anniversary, but Dad has a new wife.  Sure, like Mom, they were sealed in the Temple for Time and Eternity.  This means that Martha will be standing next to Mom, not better or worse, not over or under, but next to her as Dad's Eternal Companion.

24 years. It would've been 24 years this year if Mom hadn't died, but, in a way, I think she was meant to. I think I remember Mom saying that her Grandma Smith, a devoted member missionary, passed away before the 9/11 attacks because they'd need her over there. Maybe there's a reason Mom was taken from us so soon.

Dad still plays that memorial video playlist. At least he said he did, and Martha wept with him. I think that Martha has been so good for him because I think his heart has healed enough.

After all, he gave his heart to her. And she to him. It's refreshing, even exhilarating, to know that he found love again. I always knew he had the heart for it. He's capable of so much more.

Sara keeps commenting, when she emails me, how much they seem to be just so into each other. It's so refreshing to hear about that.

Still, both Molly and I are expecting the news that we'll be having a new sibling very soon. I mean, yeah, they're not exactly young anymore, but Martha still has a few good years, and Dad's been taking those supplements that Sara's been giving him. We expect to hear the news very soon and will be so delighted when it does happen.

October 3, 2027

I will admit, I not always the best big sister I can be.  I mean, yeah, I know Molly has her own life, but, sometimes, I can't help but be more like a mom to her, when she plainly reminds me that I'm not her mom.  It's gotten a little heated from time to time.

Friday, I waited up for her from her date.  I'll admit, I had the excuse that I had to grade homework, but it was only an excuse.  With General Conference this weekend, there's still plenty of time.

She was a full hour late.  I got a little stern with her, telling her that she should know better.  She challenged me, though, asking how many times I stayed out later than I should've been since I'm really not that much older than she is.  I mean, I'm 23, she's 17.  I admitted that, yeah, there were a few nights I stayed out late, and worried Dad sick.

I know she's not my daughter.  She's not even technically related to me, but she's still my sister.  I do tend to worry about her.

I guess that might be one of the reasons I latched onto the talks of family during this General Conference. It's such a relief, every 6 months, to be able to listen to the servants of the Lord give us guidance, and it's so refreshing to be able to hear it.

Yes, there were talks on the importance of family and how members my age should definitely find an Eternal Companion sooner or later. Molly couldn't help but mumble that it better be sooner for me, and kept that up until I reminded her that, once that happened, she'd have to go live with Martha and Dad and all their lovey dovey stuff.

But there were other talks that I kind of latched onto as well.

I listened, carefully, as a few talked about what it means, really, to be worthy. I mean, it's clear in the Scriptures that we shouldn't partake of the Sacrament without being worthy, but it's nearly impossible to go a whole week without making a mistake.

I mean, nobody's perfect on this little Earth, nobody is. Only Jesus Christ was perfect, and He had the benefit of being half-God before His Resurrection. So how could we consider ourselves worthy in His presence?

This is what I picked up on.  To be worthy isn't to be perfect.  The idea of repentance isn't only for those who commit sin. The whole idea of being penitent is that we acknowledge that we need to improve, that we need to do better.  I think it was President Nelson who pointed out that the Greek interpretation of repentance is the idea of changing, and it really is.

Sure, we make mistakes, but acknowledging them and attempting to do better is what repentance is about.  We can't go back and fix our mistakes, that's impossible.  We can't unhurt those we may have hurt.

Repentance is about wanting to do better, about making ourselves better, and, eventually, closer to Heavenly Father and Jesus Christ.  It's a lifelong process, and it needs to be cultivated.

That's what being worthy is all about, knowing that we have to change for the better and honestly striving to do so, even if it's merely the knowledge that we need to do better.

And we need to forgive.  A few years back, when I was Molly's age, someone I thought I loved very much said that forgiveness wasn't forgetting, it was merely stating that the actions done that might have hurt no longer matter.  But what more can it be?  I mean, in reality, it takes love to be able to forgive.  Sure, it's hard sometimes.  The hurt may run deep, but we need to be able to recognize that we can't unhurt.  That is where the real power leads.

So why do people find it so difficult to forgive?  I like the analogy that Dad drew up with it a few years back.  When we hold a venomous snake close, sooner or later, it will bite.  But continuing to hold onto that snake won't get the venom out.

Yet some people continue to hold onto the metaphorical snake as if it's a lifeline.  Is that the cause of the hatred epidemic?

I mean, I hear so much about those that can't let go of the past mistakes of people born way before they ever were.  I've heard people state that it's an inborn thing to hate and I have to wonder where they get that ridiculous notion.

I've seen babies smile and laugh at Dad, toddlers who have no idea who he is.  He thrills at that, but I know why it happens.  Dad is such a bright light that he can't help but be noticed, and they respond to it.

It doesn't matter that he may not be as wealthy as they are, nor even the same skin color. These young ones don't have any concept of what hate is.

Yet I've had people tell me that, because I have a paler skin, and, believe me, as a redhead my skin is permanently pale, I'm automatically racist. It's ridiculous to think like that. And, because I was born and raised in Arkansas, I'm automatically aligned with those groups that hate based on skin color. No, I've never subscribed to their ideologies.

I've had people hate me because I'm a redhead. I mean, people have honestly steered clear of me because they're afraid I'd such their souls out or something. A few years back I heard something about "kick a ginger" day and I'm like what about brunettes or blondes? Do they get their own day to be kicked?

But I don't hold grudges. I never have. Dad taught me that people who do that honestly have no idea what kind of person I am, or they'd likely come up and say hello and ask how I am. They diminish themselves by not liking me or by not wanting to know more.

So, I can forgive them easily.  I can also forgive those who, for some reason, dislike the Church of Jesus Christ of Latter-Day Saints.  Even here, in Utah, I've heard some people say some negative things about the church, but do they really know us?

Do they listen to what those who don't want to lose the money from a congregation say about a church that has no paid ministry and that has, literally, hundreds of thousands of missionaries out there that only want to spread the Gospel of Jesus Christ?

I was one of them myself.  It's not an easy life, doing that, so why do so many young people go out, into the world, and do it?

I can tell you exactly why.  The Gospel is real.  Jesus really is the Savior of us all.  It's a message for all of us, even though some may not be ready to hear it.  There are those who fight against the church, but it is the Church of Jesus Christ.  When He comes again, everything will be set right and, more than likely, all those that fought against His church will realize their mistake.

I never thought that, when they wanted to confront me in Scotland, I was fighting them.  Sure, it may have gotten tense, but I tried to keep myself calm.  When I was able to do that, the Holy Ghost was with me, and I was able to try and help their understanding come back to the Truth.

Here's where I really like what the Church of Jesus Christ of Latter-Day Saints has to offer.  We have no paid ministry.  Those who are in charge of our Wards and Branches and Stakes don't get paid for their time doing so.  Yes, we have a tithing and donation system, but it's for the upkeep of the buildings and for the helping of those who are less fortunate.  The Bishops and Stake Presidents never see a dime of it.

I think that's one of the reasons so many other "Christian" churches try and fight against us.  We tend to take away their source of money, and what did the Savior say about the love of money?

Anyway, that's what I took away from General Conference this time.  And, yes, Molly is going to keep teasing me about finding myself an Eternal Companion.

Sooner or later, I will.  I have a feeling on it.

October 5, 2027

I guess the news that I wanted to teach a form of self

defense was what prompted the school board to agree to let me do

an extracurricular class in Brazilian Jiu Jitsu.  I mean, yeah, I had to

assure them that it wasn't actually teaching the students that signed

up how to fight, because that's not what it's about, but I still wanted

to show a few moves to the first few who got in.

I was expecting, maybe, 2 or 3, maybe 4.  There were 20

girls in the gym, all suited up as I came in.  Sure, they'd get PE

credit for it, and I'd get a bonus for each student, but I really didn't

think there'd be that many interested.

I told them I needed a partner; someone I could demonstrate

on.  They assigned me Coach Mills, the PE teacher.  I'd never really

met him before, but, when I saw him, I had a bit of a nervous twinge

in my gut.  He was at least 6 foot and easily outweighed me.  But

the guys in Scotland were bigger, so I knew I could take him.

I started out this class by telling these girls the first lesson I

ever learned in Jiu Jitsu, perhaps the most important one of all.  95%

of all confrontations are won without throwing a single punch.  Sure,

I'd had to use my training battling 4 different men, and I admitted that I'd done so, but only because they left me no choice in the matter. The majority of confrontations, including the one where I'd saved my little sister, I won because I convinced the aggressor that they'd eventually lose, be embarrassed, maybe even go to jail if they went on with what they were doing.

If it's possible, and most of the time, it is, make it so that you don't have to even land a single blow. With careful wording and attitude, it's possible to win this way and make the aggressor change their minds. It's very possible that girls could defeat anyone that wanted to hurt them simply by talking to them in a manner that states they can defend themselves.

My students seemed very interested in this, but one of them, Piper, from one of my classes, raised her hand and asked what would happen the other 5%. I had to sigh and say that, yes, there are those rare times when physical confrontation is impossible.

I saw that Coach Mills seemed interested in this. He didn't seem to stop looking at me, but he was interested. I turned to him, smiling, and invited him to try and get me on my back. He was genuinely surprised at this, clearly thinking he could do it easily and stating he didn't want to hurt me.  I assured him I'd be fine and that he shouldn't be too afraid of a small redhead woman like me.

He sighed, then tried, halfheartedly, to go for me.  I had to laugh as I dodged him easily and taunt that he could do better.  I'm not sure if it was my taunting him or that the students were laughing, but he seemed to pick up steam and went for it.

A couple of moments later, I was on top of him in a grapple, holding him down.  I looked at the students and asked them to look at where my knees were.  Ryder noticed that they weren't on the ground at all, and I showed them why by inviting the coach to try and push me off of him.

I mean, yeah, I noticed that he was muscular.  I'd bet he could easily bench press me, but, when he tried, he couldn't lift me off of him.  I showed that, no matter what he did, I had easy control over every vector.

He looked me straight in the eye, and I noticed the dark blue there, and stated he'd like to get up now.  I asked him if he'd give up trying to get me on my back and he said, yeah, I proved my point.

I let him up to a round of applause and dismissed the class.  I had to shake Coach Mills' hand, giving him props for his good sportsmanship.  He asked if I'd ever actually done anything like that before and I had to tell him it was the basics, the very first lesson.  I indicated the black belt I was wearing and told him there was so much more for these students to learn.

When I got home, Molly had to ask how it went.  I told him it was a good first lesson, then she asked who they partnered me with.  When I told her it was Coach Mills, she acted all flirty and said that, yes, he was a very good-looking man.

I'll admit, I hadn't been focusing on that very much.  The class would be every Tuesday and Thursday, and, yes, I think it's going to be very interesting indeed.

But why can't I stop thinking about Coach Mills?


October 14, 2027

I thought things were progressing well in both my English classes and my Jiu Jitsu classes.  I mean, Coach Mills has been a great sport, but he still spends most of his time on his back.  I've been able to demonstrate a couple of grappling holds that totally incapacitated him.

I thought things were going well when I got another assignment back from my English students that showed, clearly, they didn't fully understand what they were reading.

Oh, sure, they gave great book reports. I got to learn a lot about the books they chose to read, even though I have to question whether or not they understand that there are some things that simply shouldn't be read, but they didn't really understand the meat of what I was trying to say.

As I handed them back today, I got down and started to tell them what it was I was really wanting from them. I told them that, sure, with math, you find out how things work. With history, you find out what happened before and what needs to be done about it. With civics, you find out about liberty and about how to preserve it. But with English, you find out about yourself through the eyes of others.

What's really essential in English Lit isn't what happens in the story. Dad's always told me this, and it's one of the reasons so many read his works, even now.  Yes, with good writing, the plot and the characters can be very charming and very relatable, but what is really the heart of any good story is the way the reader feels about it.  What does the reader glean from the story that helps them learn about themselves?  What does the reader really see in the story beyond what the words say?

As I handed back their assignments, giving them props for reporting what happened in the stories they read, I gave them another challenge, due on Monday.  Rewrite the assignment, but, this time, tell me how the story made them feel and what the story made them think.

But then the problem developed in the Jiu Jitsu class.  Sure, there were 5 others that joined, one of them a guy.  But he joined because, as he said, he wanted to learn how to fight.

I had to correct him.  Brazilian Jiu Jitsu, like most martial arts, is a form of self-defense, not a form of fighting.  If they were there to learn how to fight, then they were in the wrong afterschool class.  If they wanted to learn how to bully someone, there are other ways to find stuff like that out.

But, if they wanted to learn how to take control of a confrontation and to avoid being hurt, then they could stick around.

I figured I'd shown them enough, so I paired them off and they started to practice on each other. I had to go around, with Coach Mills following, demonstrating the correct technique as some of the girls flew, ending up on the floor. The aggressors, in many cases, were subdued, which was the whole point of the exercise.

Afterwards, Coach Mills, I think, was trying to sneak up on me after I got changed. I mean, sure, he was pretty good, but I knew he was there.

He ended up on the ground, me on top of him again, and he started laughing. He asked if I'd always been that high-strung, but I denied that I'd ever really been that. Instead, I had a sense of awareness that had developed over time.

He asked if he could get up now, so I let him up. Then he surprised me by asking what I was going to be for the Halloween dance. I shrugged, saying I hadn't planned on going.

Then he asked me to go with him. I mean, yeah, he officially asked me out. I couldn't tell if I was excited or scared, but I gave him a noncommittal answer that, if he could think of a theme for us, yes, I'd go with him.

So, I guess I have a date for a dance.


October 29. 2027

I think my classes are starting to understand what messages I'm trying to convey this semester. I'll still have most of them next semester, which means I'll be able to keep going onward without repeating anything.

But, for Halloween-time, I decided to assign them a classic of literature. Yes, a lot of them have heard of the play, but how much of the musical operetta was based on the original *Phantom of the Opera*?

I challenged them to read it and tell me what they thought about it. It's due next Friday, and I think I was kind of inspired by it.

I suggested to Coach Mills that we go to the dance as Erik, the proper name for the Phantom, and Christine. He wanted to do Cinderella and Prince Charming, but I don't think we're quite there yet.

Besides, Molly and her date already have that one, much to Martha's chagrin and Dad's amusement.

But the coach picked me up about three hours earlier. He told me that a dance wasn't a proper place to hold a conversation, not with the music blaring loudly, so he asked if he could take me to dinner first.

Molly encouraged it because she still needed time to get ready, and she thought Coach Mills' costume was particularly good for being kind of scary.

And, of all places he could've taken me, it was Olive Garden. I don't think he understood why I was laughing at the irony of it, and I'm not sure I'm ready to explain it. Still, no slips this time. Besides, he was carrying that Phantom mask with him.

He was actually surprised I'm diabetic. Here I am, a fit Type 1 diabetic that needed to get her shot before dinner, and my phone indicated that it would be fine. We talked about it for a bit, and I cleared up some misconceptions about diabetes.

I told him it's not a curse that I can never eat sugar. In fact, every person needs sugar in order to survive, as well as all the other stuff.  Diabetes isn't that it's that my body can't produce insulin anymore, and that is what is needed in order to convert sugar into cellular energy.

He did ask what it felt like to be dangerously high and dangerously low.  I told him I didn't really know what the dangerously high was, I've never been above 260.  Yes, that's high, but it's easily knocked down.  I told him that dangerous lows are far worse and that I kind of feel like I'm not really there, like I'm just kind of floating.

As we ate, we kept talking.  I found out he'd served a mission in Spain, and he seemed intrigued that my stepmom is originally from there.  He asked about Martha, of course, and asked if Mom and Dad had divorced.  I guess he realized he'd asked the wrong question when I didn't answer for a bit before I told him Mom died.  I mean, it's been almost 12 years now, and, although I think I'll miss her until I see her again, I'm very glad Dad found Martha. They're deliriously happy, which is never a bad thing.

He asked how come I know Jiu Jitsu, so I told him.  It all started when a girl where I first went to school, Boise Idaho, was killed.  Friends were terrified until I told them we could learn to defend ourselves.  That's when I ran across Brazilian Jiu Jitsu and realized it was the way to do it.

He did ask how many times I had to use it, telling me he thought I had experience in actual combat.  I told him I had and told him about my stalker in Boise.  As far as I know, or care, he's still in jail.

I told him about the three guys on my mission who were determined to teach us "little girls" a lesson.  Two of them had weapons but they were easily dispatched, the third one running away after he saw how easy I took down the other two, although I did have to spend a few weeks convalescing after one of them broke some of my ribs.

But I made it clear that, more often than not, I had used persuasion to get people to back down.  I never did like hurting people.

He asked if that meant him, to which I laughed and said that I'd never intended to hurt him in all the times I've taken him down, only get him to give up.  I did say that, sooner or later, I'd probably have to show how to completely incapacitate him, to which he had a strange kind of smile.

I guess I should explain the dance. Being in Utah, basically the home state of the Church of Jesus Christ of Latter-Day Saints, the Halloween Dance was held in conjunction with the church dance at the Stake Center. This means it wasn't just high school students but also middle-school students as well. And there were a lot of costumes.

And we weren't the only grown-ups there either. Aside from a good portion of youth leaders, obviously working as chaperones, there were a few other teachers there as well.

It wasn't until about halfway through when Ryan, as Coach Mills insisted I call him from now on, asked if I knew how to swing dance. I had to laugh, tell him yes, but to be very careful on the lifts. He asked me what I meant but I only told him I'd tell him later.

So, yeah, a few other couples were swing dancing as well, and Ryan was honestly surprised at how well I was handling being spun around him. He did try and lift me once, and didn't drop me, not like that first time.

Anyway, as he dropped me off back at home, he said he had a great time, which I echoed.  He did say he wanted to do something with me again soon, so I had to say I was going to be doing a ghost hunt tomorrow and invited him along.

Not like a date or anything.  Not like tonight.

I don't know, but this might lead to something more.


October 30, 2027

Tonight was kind of interesting.  Ryan, Molly, two of her friends and myself all went on a ghost hunt at the Union Station here in Ogden.  I thought that, since it's been officially closed for 30 years, they might not be open to the idea of having a ghost hunting group in there, but they've allowed groups like mine in there for many, many years.

Before we went in, Ryan, being Coach Mills again, acted all tough and everything, saying he'd protect us girls.  I had to laugh.  I told all of them the facts as I knew them, that ghosts are, for the most part, simply people without bodies.

Yes, they can be a bit disturbing, even startling.  Sure, the cold spots that sneak up on you don't help, neither do the other phenomena that occur.  I even told them one of Dad's theories, that the EMF fluctuations that are present with spiritual activity, one that just feeds the ghost, may very well add to the unease we feel in their presence.

Molly didn't act afraid, but her friends were nervous.  Erin and Kris both looked around, a little afraid, when we went in.

I had the girls download some apps to their phones, EVP recorders, thermal imagers, the like.  I had the Spirit Box app on my phone on as we went in.

I will admit, it felt a little eerie.  I mean the place hasn't been used in 30 years, officially.  Sure, it's a tourist trap now, and ghost hunters come in all the time, but I had to know.  I asked if there was anyone with us tonight.

I got an answer that stated that, of course, there was.  Erin nearly jumped out of her skin at that, looking around nervously.  She had to know where that voice came from on my phone.  Ryan put a hand on her shoulder, trying to calm her, and just said the voice couldn't hurt her.

I was kind of proud of him for that, although I don't know if it was as a teacher or a coach.  Or maybe just being a human being.  I told Erin that, even if it is unnerving, there are only a few ghosts out there that can actually harm the living.  Sure, they get a lot of media attention and there are so many YouTube channels and TV shows about ghosts, but, for the most part, they just want to be able to talk to us.

My Spirit Box confirmed that, so I had to ask the ghost that was speaking to us its name.  Came back as a David, someone who died on the rail platform sometime in the 1940s.  He was one of only 3 ghosts that were there, all of them victims of accidents, but they didn't mind that they were remembered this way.

Ryan and I looked at each other for a moment, wondering what would be going on, before one of the other spirits came forward with something that sounded like "kiss."

Molly giggled at that, watching me intently.  I suggested that the lady that requested that was, instead, saying "kids," trying to deflect away from the sudden awkwardness, and trying to reference them.

I mean, yeah, I like Ryan.  He's a good sport and a great support, and I want to spend more time with him when I can, but I don't think we're at the stage of kissing yet.

But who knows?


November 8, 2027

Okay, so, some of the Jiu Jitsu class noticed that something had changed between Ryan and me.  I mean, it's not obvious or anything, but I guess it was a bit different that we started greeting each other by our first names instead of Coach Mills and Ms. Thurber.  I don't know where it's going, but I hope it keeps going there.

And, today, I handed back the reports for *Phantom of the Opera*.  I had to admit, to my classes, that I was kind of impressed how they took what I wanted and applied it to the story.  About 80% of them had to acknowledge that Sir Andrew Lloyd Weber didn't follow the original story very closely at all.  It was more of an homage to the original but took heavy liberties.

Gaston Leroux's original work didn't take place in some fictional theater, it took place in the world-famous Paris Opera House.  And there were more than a few who asked if the story might be based on a real event.

I had to give them good marks for that question, because it's been one of mine for a long time, ever since I first read it.  I mean, sure, in the days it was written, those with deformities and disabilities were thought of as monsters, so it's not a big leap to say that one person, probably a genius, with a deformed face, might have hidden away across that underground lake under the Paris Opera House.

I had to ask, though, why they thought it might not just be a work of fiction, and, I think, Mick said it best when he said that it's rare for fiction writers to focus everything on the unearthing of a skeleton.  I told him, and the rest of that class, that Dad had written an entire series on a dream he had way before any of them were born, so why was it remarkable that the skeleton discovered seemed to bring out a work of fiction?

I pointed out, to all my classes, the sad truth that, during that time, yes, many with deformities were thought of as monsters.  But were they?

I've met people with Down's Syndrome.  Yes, their faces aren't the same as ours and, yes, their capacities aren't the same, but I've never known more angelic people ever.  It's like their disability gives them a step towards the fact that, in the eyes of Heaven, every one of us is a child of God.

So would Erik, the eponymous phantom, really have hidden away from the world?  Would he have fallen in love with the beautiful Christine and wanted her to be his forever?  Would he really have tortured the original Raul to get him to stop loving her?

Someone pointed out, in pretty much every class, that Raul fell into the torture pit with the Persian.  It wasn't originally Erik's plan, but Christine did save Raul the same way as in the operetta, by promising to stay with Erik.

And it was that one act of human kindness that changed him. So how many times would the simple act of being kind to someone who might feel left out work for them? How much would it cost to simply say hello to someone or give someone a smile who seems to be feeling down?

I didn't know if I reached anyone, not until I got that email tonight. It simply read that whoever sent it was thinking of running away until I said those things.

I guess I'm going to be that kind of teacher then.


November 25, 2027

So today was Thanksgiving and thank goodness it's over with. I mean, it wasn't bad, but Ryan's sisters were all insisting on going out and checking the sales for the evening.

Yeah, we spent the day at the Mills', and I can tell you that I think that they were trying to impress us. Or maybe not. I still don't know just yet.

It turns out that Ryan's grandfather was someone who set up a car lot in Ogden a few decades ago. It was thought that some of these cars were going to just be a fad, but he had an instinct.

They actually live in the town of Roy, a short drive outside of Ogden. Or, rather, they live on the outskirts of Roy, on a freakin' ranch.

At least it looked like a ranch. I mean, Molly and I drove for at least 30 minutes before we found the house, and it was big. I thought the Chamberlain house in McCall was big, but this one simply towered over us. I felt myself shudder a little bit. What was I getting myself into here?

Honestly, we passed a herd of cows on the drive in here, and I think I know whose they are now.

Anyway, we got up to the front entrance and rang the bell. I fully expected a butler or someone to answer the door, but it was Ryan. He hugged both of us like we were the last guests to arrive, and I think we may have been.

Ryan introduced us, and his sisters, Marie and Carlie, had to just sit me down and ask everything about me. Molly just kind of sat there as they interrogated me, wondering what kind of girl their brother had found so interesting he invited her out here.

I had to indicate he invited both Molly and me, to which they reached out and touched Molly's legs, welcoming her as well. It was Carlie who looked between us for a moment and pointed out that we didn't look anything alike. I laughed as Molly explained that we're stepsisters but couldn't be closer if we'd both been born to the same parents.

So, Marie had to know how that came about. I told them how Mom died shortly after I turned 11, and how Dad basically put himself in cold storage for years afterwards. Molly perked up then and told them that her mom and Dad met, then. How it was practically love at first sight with them.

Molly's dad died a few years ago as well, she explained. But now, we're all one big family in the Lord's eyes.

Finally, I got a chance to ask about this spread of land we'd driven onto. Yes, it's a ranch, about a thousand acres big. No, they don't all live in the big house. Marie and Carlie both have their own places, with their families, on the ranch grounds, and, when Ryan finds the right one, he'll have his own place as well.

A few kids came in, although I couldn't tell which kids belonged to which sister and said that dinner would be about ready. Molly and I brought a bean casserole, but it was so lost in the bewildering buffet that lay before us. Sister Mills had us all bow our heads as Brother Mills, or Father Mills as he wanted to be called, pronounced the blessing on the dinner. Honestly, I thought Dad said long prayers.

I had managed to take my insulin beforehand, and Molly and I managed to get all the forks and spoons in the right order, but we were so stuffed afterwards. I mean _STUFFED_. I know there's a popular Thanksgiving urban myth that the tryptophan in the turkey makes you sleepy, but I found out, only a couple of years ago, that there's not enough to knock anyone out. It's carbohydrate overload.

I managed to look at my Dexcom reading, and it did say I had enough insulin in me to balance everything out. I kind of bragged that I knew how to make the best hot chocolate ever, which had Carlie say that, for Christmas, I'd have to make it.

So, I guess we know where we're coming for Christmas. Dad and Martha will have to make do on their own, although I don't think they'd even notice we're not there.


December 7, 2027

It's kind of nuts right now at school. Everyone, students and teachers both, is eagerly awaiting Winter Break. I mean, I don't know why they don't just call it Christmas Vacation. It happens around Christmas, but I guess someone didn't want those who don't believe that Jesus is the Christ to be offended.

But that's their problem. I still celebrate Christmas, and Molly and I are going to figure something out.

At least we were. After the Jiu Jitsu class today, Ryan just casually mentioned that his family would be doing their usual Christmas tradition. I kind of took the hint that he wanted to ask me to join them, well, Molly and me. I had to mention how his sisters would probably get a hint that there was something deeper going on between us and how they'd probably try their best to get us together outside of the ranch house.

Ryan laughed, but then surprised me when he said they usually spent Christmas skiing at Snowbasin Lodge outside of Huntsville.  That surprised me, but then it surprised me more when he finally asked if Molly and I would like to join them.

I guess I knew this was coming.  I mean, I knew it.  I had to tell him that I'd never been skiing in my life, so I wouldn't know what to do.  He told me he knew of a place that had a skiing simulator and wondered if I'd like to join him there, Saturday, to actually pick up a few key pointers.

I had to laugh.  I mean, officially, he's only asked me out once.  But wouldn't this be our *fourth* date?  He looked at me funny before I explained the reasoning behind that.

Yes, he asked me to the Halloween dance, then we went on that ghost hunting adventure, then there was Thanksgiving, and now he wants me to join him at the gym.  And wait, there's a fifth one as well, at the ski lodge.

He admitted I had a point, but then smiled and asked if that would make us boyfriend and girlfriend now.  I put a hand on his arm and told him to just cool his jets.

I'm not sure just yet.


December 11, 2027

For the record, I do have a gym membership.  Hey, I like to keep fit, and I know that it's a part of what makes me feel better after a rough day.  It helps when the depression and anxiety get bad.

I also have a Brazilian Jiu Jitsu place I keep training at, even though I'm already a black belt.  I'm honestly training two classes, in effect, which is great.

But I hadn't been to Ryan's gym.  I hadn't even seen it until he gave me directions to go there today.  I mean, okay, he did invite me so that I could try out the ski simulator there.

When he greeted me, he did kind of surprise me with a big hug.  I guess it's expected on the 4th date, so I returned it.  He took me back, signing me in as a guest, and showed me the simulator.

Pressure, angles, momentum.  Body position.  All these things came to mind as I saw the thing and just understood it.  I stood on a platform, toes pointed inward, and just let the simulator run.

At least that's what I understood when I saw it.  There wasn't any real danger present, but I had to ask if that was it.  Ryan assured me it was, but that he'd watch and make sure I did it right.

So, I sighed, kind of belaying my confidence.  I mean, I understood it almost immediately before I got up there⋯.

And fell right off.  Ryan helped me back up and I knew what I did wrong before he asked if my balance was okay.  I assured him it was, then stood up on it again.  It was a lot more delicate than it looked, which I didn't consider.

Getting on the platform was easy.  Getting my feet in position was easy, even though I kind of laughed, not knowing why I was having a hard time with it.  I asked Ryan to start it and was presented with a mountain of snow.  I gasped as things just kind of came at me.

I mean, it was easy for me to understand.  Lean from side to side to steer.  Be able to move around objects that way and use the poles to help.  The poles on the simulator were attached and could be moved very easy.

But, for some reason, I just couldn't concentrate as I ran into the first simulated tree.  I scoffed at it, then insisted I go again.  Ran into another tree this time.

I mean, I understood the physics of it.  I understood the design of it.  I could do it, but, for some reason, I just couldn't then.

Ryan finally got behind me, off the platform, and suggested he help me out.  As we started again, he put his hands on my hips and tried to show me how to steer.  I felt him pressing, guiding my hips as we went down the simulated mountain until we reached the base.

I honestly can't tell you why, but I jumped off, hugging him, as we finished that run.  He held me a moment longer before I suggested we try it again.

After that second run, I told him I thought I could do it on my own this time, even though it was clear he wanted to keep helping me.  I did just fine the third time, just doing what I thought needed to be done.

After a couple more runs, Ryan declared I was ready to try real skis and emphasized that Molly and I were invited up to Snowbasin for Christmas.

As I told Molly about what happened a little later, she had a dreamy look in her eyes, asking what it felt like to be "steered" by Ryan.  I had to make something up and tell her it was because I usually ended up putting him on the floor two days a week, so I wanted him to feel better.

But why was my heart still racing?  Why was it that, even hours later, I still felt his hand on my hips?  Why am I smiling so much?


December 25, 2027

So, yeah, it's Christmas.  We're here, at Snowbasin Resort, and I don't think I've ever seen so much snow in my life.  Marie has been something of a mother hen to Molly, which I thought was funny.

Sure, I had to rent my skis, and it seemed like a totally different ballgame from the simulator, but it was *such a rush* when I finally got on the hill.  Sure, they wanted me to start out on the

beginner hill, so I did, with Molly.

I can't tell you what it felt like with the wind going through

my hair as I flew down the hill.  I'm not sure exactly how fast I was

going, but I was laughing the whole way down.

The Mills' had everything set up today.  I'm not sure how

they managed to do it, but they had skis and boots all ready for

Molly and me, our own sets.

We're not the only ones up here, though.  There are three

other families, but we're all kind of hanging out together.  I had

some fun getting the family's Christmas Chocolate together, just as

Dad made it.  Carlie seemed so surprised, almost giddy at the idea

of actual melted chocolate in warmed milk and eggnog together.

She and her kids seemed intent on trying to help out when I told

them it needs constant stirring.

I warned her youngest, as I served him, that it was very rich,

but to use the candy cane to stir it as he sipped.  He almost gagged

when he decided to try a deep swallow.  His mom just patted his

back and said he'd better listen to "Aunt Aurelia" next time.

"Aunt Aurelia?" That title took me by surprise. I mean, yeah, they made me feel right at home, with the nice clothes and everything they got us. They didn't laugh when I slipped that one time up on the slope and were honestly impressed that I knew how to ski. I had to tell them I'd never worn them before in my life, but Marie didn't believe me.

Molly did okay herself. I mean, she is my kid sister and all that. I do forget, sometimes, we're not technically related. I mean, it's like we were raised together, even though our parents only married each other about 6 months ago.

I honestly don't know how they managed to bring all that food up here, but dinner was excellent. I knew what I had to do for my diabetes and did it.

And then Ryan asked me what I knew about pool. I had to laugh. It was such a repeat performance because I knew how to play, and I could play very well from the moment I was introduced to the actual game.

I decided to hustle him a little bit.  It was supposed to be that kind of relationship, and, well, I kind of started off losing the first game on purpose.  I know how I did, and I know what I did.

But Molly had to smirk at me as Ryan "helped me" with the first couple of shots.  Yes, his arms were around me, and, although I already knew how to line it up, I had to bite my bottom lip to keep from giggling like a schoolgirl.  It felt so good.

And then I revealed my hand with the third game.  He bet me that, if I could sink the 8 ball before him, he'd kiss me.  I asked what would happen if he won, to which he only smiled.

He knew he'd been hustled then.  I proceeded to make shot after shot, even explaining how I was going to do it as I went.  He accused me of already knowing how to play well, and I reminded him he'd never really asked.  He just assumed.

As the 8 ball went in, I dropped my stick on the table, trembling a little.  Was he going to do it?  Was he going to pay off?

Was it going to be just because of the bet?  I mean, yeah, I've been thinking about him a lot.  I've tried to make sure I don't hurt him when we're teaching that class together at school.

I know he's a good guy, a member of the church and a returned missionary.  I know he's good with his family.  Sure, his family has money, but that doesn't matter so much to me.

What was he going to do?  I mean, I've been kissed before. It's been a while, but I have been.  What would this mean for us? What was going to happen?

As he walked over to me, he took my shoulders gently and told me he'd been wanting to do this since we first met.  I was breathing deeply, not sure what was going to happen, before he gently stroked my face, sliding his hand behind my neck and bringing my lips to his.

I felt myself explode into a ball of flame.  Every part of me was on fire, burning hot.  I melted like a stick of butter on a hot plate, no longer solid.

I could almost feel the turn of the Earth beneath me and the movement of the stars themselves.  Where was I again?  It didn't matter.  All I knew was this, Ryan.  All I wanted to know was Ryan.

I was at one with him, we were the same.  Everything was the same and nothing else came close.  We were the only ones in the universe, the only ones who mattered.

Somewhere, I heard someone moan in contentment and happiness.  After the second one, I realized it was me.  I've been kissed before, and felt what I thought was happiness before, but this seemed to eclipse them all.

After a moment, or was it a thousand years, Ryan's lips parted from mine, and I could feel myself trying to catch my breath.  He held me close, just holding onto me, as I heard him whisper that he loves me.

I cuddles a little closer as I whispered that I know, and he laughed as he accused me of pulling a Han/Leia thing.  I had to laugh as well.  Yes, although I'm not sure just yet, I do think I love him.

It was only then that we realized we weren't alone.  Molly had been filming the whole thing and, before I could get to her, sent it to Dad.

I swiped at her before she laughed and told me she thought Dad would so approve.

Turns out she was right.  Dad and Martha were both cheering as they responded to Molly's message.  I had to admit, it did feel good.  It feels so good to be wanted like that again.


January 3, 2028

I mean, I do like Ryan.  Sure, most of the time we teach together, I'm beating him up, but he always makes me feel safe.  He's interested in what I have to offer and he's interesting.

And, yes, we did share a New Year's kiss in front of everyone, which had Marie and Carlie both cheering.  I think that we could have something together.

I just don't know if I'm in love with him like he is with me.  I do know I like it when he's around and Molly's always saying how his presence makes me smile.  Maybe there is a connection there, I just don't know yet.

Maybe I'm just a little guarded after that whole deal with my heart being broken on my mission.  I do have a therapist here, so maybe she can help me work through this.

Am I ready to be in love again?

That's a question for another day.  Today, I started the next

semester reading one of Dad's favorite plays.  I think they're

starting to get the message I'm trying to convey in my classroom,

because a couple of the girls thought it was so fitting that we read

*Cyrano de Bergerac*.

I asked all my classes to try and explain what they thought

was the most romantic play of all.  Many said *Romeo and Juliet*, but I

corrected them in telling them it is basically a story of stupidity.

Romeo is just a young man given to passions, given to stalking, and

Juliet is a much younger girl who hasn't really had enough

experiences in her life to justify what happened.

If it were to happen today, for example, Romeo would face

jail time for Statutory Rape and Juliet would probably be grounded

until she's 30.

No, if you want to see something truly romantic, take a look

at *Cyrano de Bergerac.*  I told them that we were going to start the

play tomorrow, and that the whole thing would probably take until

Spring Break.  I'd assign the roles based on who I thought was the most deserving each day and ask them what their opinion of the scenes were after we were done.

I think I had their interest, then.  I'm trying to keep them interested in the overall lesson I'm trying to teach.


February 14, 2028

I'm almost positive Dad and Martha are celebrating today, just like they celebrated his birthday.  Honestly, I think I made the right decision, asking Molly to move in with me over here and leaving those two lovebirds alone.  And I know Dad told Martha why he's not a big fan of Valentine's Day.

I think I timed it just right, in my class, with the play.  I mean, sure, at first, some of the girls in my class claimed that Roxanne was "incredibly shallow" to fall for a guy based only on his looks, but I reminded them to just be patient.  The truth of it all would come out later, and the characters will actually grow.  I promised them that.

But, today, we focused on the real balcony scene.  Sure, when most people think of a romantic balcony scene, they think of

*Romeo and Juliet,* but I asked the class to consider what the difference was in this one.

It was one of the guys that spotted it first, and, I'll admit, I was kind of proud of him for it. The main difference was that, in *Cyrano,* there was actual dialog. True, Cyrano was able to express how he really feels about Roxanne under the guise of being Christian, and practically wooed her, taking comfort in the fact that, when Christian was up there, getting his kiss, it was Cyrano's words that did that, basically she was kissing his words.

Chelsea actually had a point when her hour was there. Although Cyrano loved Roxanne, it was basically from a distance. He treated her well, even did a little bit of playing with her, and listened to her. He treated her like a *person* who had her own hopes and dreams, not like something to be obsessed over or something to try and steal. One of the other girls caught on and said that, yeah, women aren't objects or prizes to be won, we're people, every bit as much as guys. I had to bring that forward to all my classes today, even though there were a few guys who were clearly uncomfortable with it.

But when Ryan asked me out tonight, I had to tell him no.  I mean, ever since January, we've been out quite a few times.  He's so fun, so comforting, so safe.  I believe I am falling for him hard.

But, when he asked, I told him.  I told him I don't really do Valentine's Day with all the chintz and pretentiousness.  I told him that, for me and the man I end up marrying, there should be more than just one day a year devoted to romance.  He seemed to take comfort it that but was honestly sad when I told him it's also when Mom got so sick and died 5 days later.

He wants to celebrate Mom's life with me on the 19th, so I said yes.  He also said he has something in mind that will probably make that day a little bit more bearable.

I think he's going to propose.


February 19, 2028

12 years today.  And, honestly, if it wasn't for Dad's playlist, I think I would've forgotten Mom's face and voice by now.  I mean, yes, I have a stepmom who loves me, but Martha told me, many times, that she's not going to try and replace Mom, just like, even

though she's legally adopted by Dad, he's not going to try and take the place of Molly's real dad.

But I have a new mom and a new sister. I'm positive Mom sent them our way because we'd need them. And I think we needed them today.

I found myself talking to Martha about Ryan a lot. It actually surprised me when Martha told me I sounded like I was very much in love. I had to ask her what she meant, and she told me about how often I mentioned Ryan. No longer Coach Mills, but Ryan. And I always had a smile when I talked about him, so it meant there was something there I hadn't actually been able to tell yet.

Or maybe I was afraid to. I mean, it's been almost 2 months since Ryan told me he loves me, and, although I kind of wanted to, I haven't had the courage to say it back.

At least not until tonight.

Ryan took me out, kind of surprising me, wearing a black armband and looking pretty nice. I mean, he's only a year older than I am, but he does clean up nice.

He took me to one of the nicest restaurants in Ogden, wanting me to have a good memory of today, or so he claimed. I mean, he did seem kind of nervous about the whole thing, being very quiet, before he asked me about my memories of Mom.

I told him about all her crochet genius, how she seemed to just pick it up out of nowhere. I told him about how I inherited her red hair, but she had the fiery temper. I told him about nights when she'd have to come in and break up Dad tickling me.

I told him about the night she died, about how Dad wouldn't let me see her, before finally telling me what had happened. It was a heart attack, way too early. And how, it seemed, every February 19 was a solemn day.

He grinned then, telling me that, maybe, today didn't have to be so solemn. Without any preamble, Ryan video dialed a number on his phone and set it up before taking my hands and inviting me to stand by the table.

As I stood, unsure but hoping, Ryan stood with me, telling me something I don't think I'll ever forget. "Aurelia Delyn Thurber, you are a bright and shining star. You make the whole area around you a better place just by being in it, and I want you to do that forever⋯with me."

He dropped to one knee, pulling out a box with black fur on it and opening it. Inside was a ring with a shiny clear stone on top.

He presented it to me with these words. "Aurelia, would you do me the high honor of becoming my Eternal Companion?"

I didn't know I was weeping. I just knew I was hyperventilating, or at least I thought it was that. I just knew I was nodding, saying yes.

He slipped the ring on my finger as he stood and I threw my arms around him, finally telling him that I love him.

There were cheers all around, but that didn't matter then. All I knew was him. All I knew was that I wanted him to be mine forever.

That's when I heard a familiar gruff voice. Dad was on the phone. I don't know how Ryan got his number, but he was there, and he was demanding something of my fiancé. Did he think he was worthy of me?

Ryan humbly bowed his head and said, no, he didn't.  But he'd do everything he could to be worthy of me, everything.

Dad laughed, told him he liked him and then congratulated us both as did Martha.

And, when Molly saw the ring on my finger, she flung her arms around me, jumping up and down.

Fiancée.  I like that title.


February 22, 2028

So, here I've been a fiancée for three days today, and I have had quite a few reactions to it.  All the girls in my classes were so delighted that I'm wearing a ring now.  I mean *all of them,* even those that clearly don't think it's worth the time to have one.

And, so, today, I get to my classroom and there is a huge bouquet of flowers on my desk, red carnations, I think.  I haven't really gotten into flowers yet, with a card that stated the sender would see me later and he was looking forward to our class together.  I knew who it was, naturally, so I just slipped the card into my desk before the classes started.

Chelsea thought the flowers really added to the whole aesthetic of the room, as did a few of the other girls, before one of them asked a rather interesting question that I decided needed to be addressed to everyone today.  In *Cyrano,* why didn't Cyrano just pluck up the courage and tell Roxanne how he felt?  I mean, it's pretty clear to everyone who's reading the play in the classes *and loving it.*

Yes, I replied, Cyrano is very brave.  He faced down a hundred men (okay, only 8) in defense of a friend of his.  This is the sign of someone who's unafraid of anything, so why didn't he just tell Roxanne he was in love with her?

I looked around at the class and asked them, without any request for an answer, how many of them thought they were good enough?  How many of them looked in the mirror and saw something they'd like to have changed?  How many of them compared themselves to some unattainable stretch of "perfection" that was displayed for them?

What if our own perceived shortcomings prevented us from reaching for something we wanted?  What if what we wanted wasn't easy to get so we just gave up?

I pointed out how, in the first act, Cyrano, after winning a duel in rhyme, declared that he saw the reason why he would never find love every time he saw his profile in silhouette.  What happens with that?  Don't we all see some shortcoming in us?

I mean, didn't I think I was cursed to never find love?  I know I thought that way for a while, but here I am, engaged to be married.

I didn't say that to the classes, though.  I knew I'd thought that way before and that my own insecurities kept me from telling Ryan how much I love him.

Speaking of Ryan, he asked how I liked my surprise when we did the Jiu Jitsu class, but then had a puzzled look on his face.  He actually asked me if I'd lost my ring or if I'd changed my mind because I wasn't wearing it.

I just told him that I didn't want to scratch him up with it and that it was safely back, locked in my desk in my classroom, and that I'd get it later.

He just held me for a minute, thinking that was a great idea, before a couple of giggled brought us back to the class.

I like that, he held me.


April 2, 2028

I mean, I had an idea of everything that would go into a wedding, I helped plan two of them, but the pressure of actually being the bride is something I wasn't entirely aware of.

I mean, sure, everything had to be settled on, *everything.* Two weekends ago, we had to go ring shopping. I told Ryan I was fine with just wearing the ring he gave me when he proposed, but he wanted everything to be perfect for his one true love. He knows that I don't expect perfection, I just expect him to be there for me.

The color palette was easy, even though Ryan's sisters tried to talk me into other colors, I decided on red and gold. And then they promised they were going to take me gown shopping.

I mean, it's not like I'm really going to get married in it. It'll be Temple clothes and robes, not some fancy dress that cost way too much.  I kept telling them I live on a teacher's salary, but they promised they'd take care of it.

And, of course, this weekend is General Conference.  It's also the start of Spring Break, which is why I wanted to time my classes perfectly, to kind of build things up.  It was at the point, in the battlefield, when Christian demanded that Cyrano tell Roxanne that it was he, not Christian, who wrote her those letters that so totally won her heart.  He wanted to give Roxanne the choice.

I managed to time it pretty well, so well that a lot of my students were demanding that I tell them who Roxanne chose.  I simply bid them a good Spring Break, although I think that many of them are going to skip ahead and find the answer.

We spent the weekend out on the ranch, though.  Sure, there are plenty of guest rooms, but Father Mills insisted that Ryan and I sleep on opposite sides of the house.  They have motion detectors in the middle, so that'd keep us from trying to sneak in to see each other.

But I told him that wasn't a problem.  Both of us had promised, a long time ago, to keep the law of chastity.  Sure, a particular point of that law was gong to apply only to us soon, but we were going to keep it.  That was something we promised not only ourselves but each other.

It didn't mean that Ryan wasn't rubbing my back before I went to bed.  Molly was always watching, a little doe eyed, just interested in all that was happening between us.  Ryan would always try to make sure I was comfortable, even though this house was huge.

But, after the sessions today, I got a call from someone I hadn't heard from in years.  Faye Chamberlain actually called me up and *chewed me out* for not even thinking of her when it came time to design gowns for myself and my potential bridesmaids.  I honestly hadn't even decided on who I'd ask to stand in for that.

Yes, General Conference was good, uplifting and enlightening.  More temples were announced, no surprise there, in places all over, and Ryan and I just held each other's hands at talks of Eternal Families.  There were plenty of talks to the youth of the church and quite a few on the Savior and His Sacrifice.  It is Easter, today, so that kind of ties in.

I guess I'm spending a week with my future in-laws, but, hey, I love them, so that's fine.


April 9, 2028

Molly was a bit of a surprise this Fast Sunday.  I mean, sure, it's usually the first Sunday of the month, when members of the Church of Jesus Christ of Latter-Day Saints fast for two meals on a day and give the proceeds of what that meal may have cost to the church to help those who aren't as fortunate.  It's been a few years since I've actually been able to fast like that, but I still donate.

It's also Testimony meeting today, where members who feel inclined can go up and bear their testimonies of the Gospel of Jesus Christ, no assignment, no pressure, except from the Holy Ghost. Molly got up, saying how grateful she has been that she has a big sister now, one that has watched out for her for a while now.  She gave a brief rundown of how we became sisters, even getting a few laughs in from the congregation.

And then the other surprise happened, just out of the blue.  I heard a voice from the past address me as Sister Thurber, a voice I hadn't heard in about 4 years, a voice with a very familiar accent.

I turned around, surprised to see Bethany McCall there, looking as radiant as I've ever seen her, with a black nametag on her dress.

I called her by her first name, and she corrected me by pointing to her nametag, smiling the whole while.  Of course, we had to hug and go and sit down for a while, her companion patiently waiting.  I had to hear all the news from Kirkintolloch.  I still like that name.

Betha… Sister McCall told me everything, how the little branch has grown, and then mentioned something I hadn't forgotten about at all.

She did have a relapse a short time after she got out of rehabilitation, but then pulled something out of her bag.  She let me see it, claiming her companion was there to celebrate with her.  It was a 3-year sobriety chip.  She only got it the last week.

I hugged her again and she asked if I still was Sister Thurber.  She indicated the ring on my finger, and I told her that it'd happen in a couple of months.  In fact, we'd already set a date.

July 17, my birthday, always seemed like a great day for couples to be married.  She asked if it was the guy I'd been attached to when I was there, in Scotland, but I told her, no, he'd married someone else.

Anyway, we talked for a good 20 minutes before they had to go to an appointment.  Molly was patiently waiting, as patient as an 18-year-old can be, so I told her about Bethany McCall and how, when I was in Scotland, I'd basically saved the life of a messed up, addicted kid who promised, after everything else, she'd be going on a mission.

I honestly never expected to be in her presence again but am so glad she found me today.


May 22, 2028

I had quite a few of my girls in tears last Thursday.  No, not the Jiu Jitsu class, my regular classes.  We finished *Cyrano de Bergerac*, including that very climactic death scene for Cyrano.

The whole thing started off as a comedy, you see.  Cyrano was a very larger-than-life character who dared to try to influence people.  He was a philosopher, a romantic, a dreamer, a rogue, a soldier and, of course, a writer.  The only really obnoxious thing about him, though, was his rather large nose.

But the play went on, where his love interest, his old friend and cousin Roxanne, had a crush on a good-looking soldier in his regiment.  She asked Cyrano to watch out for him, which he did, only to find out that Christian had a rather dull wit, except when it came time to aggravate Cyrano.

He took Christian under his wing so that he could help him woo Roxanne, promising him that Cyrano would write Roxanne in Christian's name.  This is what led to before that great balcony scene, where Christian, with his dull wit, tried to talk to Roxanne on his own and completely failed.

Then Christian tried again, at Roxanne's balcony, with Cyrano's guidance before Cyrano decided to take matters into his own hands, completely wooing the woman both of them loved.  As their regiment commandeer, a little vindictive that Christian and Roxanne had been married, told both Cyrano and Christian they were going to the front lines, Roxanne begged Cyrano to watch out for him and protect him.  She also asked that he get Christian to write.

Every day, since then, twice a day, Cyrano would pen a letter to Roxanne and send it off, even going through enemy lines to deliver it.  It was during a low point, when food and morale were very low in the regiment, that they had a surprise visit from Roxanne, one with a wagonload of food.  That's when Roxanne told Christian that she didn't care about his looks anymore, that she cared for his soul more.  Christian found out Cyrano had been sending the letters and demanded that Cyrano tell Roxanne the truth so that she could decide which man she loved more.

He just about did before Christian was attacked and killed, when Cyrano lied to him and told him that Roxanne chose him.  She never made that choice, you see.

For years afterwards, Roxanne mourned the death of Christian, only being visited by some of her old courtiers that still cared about her, including her favorite, Cyrano.

Then, one day, he was a little late.  There was a good reason for that, too.  He tried his usual bit of humor, trying to at least cheer her up some, before asking to read the last letter Christian wrote her, the one stained with his blood⋯and Cyrano's tears.  Even as the light was fading, Cyrano read it.  Even when it was too dark, he finished it and Roxanne knew.

This was before a couple of Cyrano's friends ran in to find him, Roxanne astonished that she had her soulmate with her the whole time.  Right before he died in a very dramatic scene.

So, I had my class write what they thought of the play, what their impressions were of it.  The majority were actually quite sad, wanting to know what Cyrano was really thinking in those final moments.  Many of the girls actually got the point of the play, and I went with that.

Today, I told them what I thought of the play, that here was someone who had a slight abnormality, but to compensate for it, he had an enormous personality.  And, yet he still didn't quite feel he deserved the love he sought.

And why?  Was he afraid?  Well, yes.  And how many of us are afraid that, somehow, a perceived inadequacy in us will be discovered and we'll be judged and even laughed at?  How many of us look at others and think that, just by one view, we know everything about them?

Sure, it's easy to get friends.  It's very easy for some.  They have the personalities that draw people to them, but what about the others?

What about the introvert in the corner?  What about the person who doesn't speak up much because they don't think they have anything interesting to say?

Aren't their voices important too?  It's not just the ones who say things in big crowds that have important things to say, it's the quiet ones that really make the most difference.

And how valuable are these people?  In the sight of God, who's the most valuable one of them all?  Aren't we all His children?  Doesn't that mean He values us all the same?

What would it accomplish if we decided to pay a little more attention to those who are outside of our normal groups?  How much good could be done if we included people we normally wouldn't include?

For Roxanne, she very much fell in love with a beautiful soul.  It was too late when she found out who that soul belonged to, but what would have changed if she would've discovered that Cyrano's soul was the beautiful one she'd longed for?  Sure, there was the attraction factor, but, after that, it got to the important parts.

Physical bodies age.  They change.  That can't be helped.  Sure, there's a whole range of medical practices that tries to stop it, but, in the end, that gets expensive and, to be blunt, obvious.

But what's really important is the soul connection, and not just to the ones we love.  And what would happen if we had that kind of connection not because of how someone looks, but because we know they're valuable too?

I left my classes with that today.  I mean, I do think that's the lesson Dad picked up when Cyrano became his favorite play.  I think I'm going to emphasize this a little more by showing these classes "Roxanne," and, maybe, the old French version of "Cyrano" with Gerard Depardieu.  I don't know how many of them take French, but it should be interesting.

I just got a few emails that really surprised me.  I mean, they're all anonymous.  I don't even know who sent them.  A few of them said they're going to try and be more outgoing to people that they'd never thought of before.  I had at least 3 that said they'd been contemplating suicide, but this one really surprised me.

This student told me they'd been thinking of bringing a gun to school and shooting a few people.  My talking about the value of souls changed this person's mind as they can't see themselves ending souls just because they're frustrated.  They're going to seek

help, instead.

As I closed those emails out, I couldn't help but remember

that vision I had on my mission, the one where my pond, instead of

just having ripples, had tsunamis.  Is this what it meant?  Have I

changed all these people's lives for the better, and they, in turn, will

change others?

That's an incredible thought.


June 9, 2028

The past week has been very interesting.  I mean, I had no

idea how much *fun* I'd have grading finals.  Molly thinks I'm a

weirdo, but that's okay because, when I try to see things from her

perspective, it is weird to like grading papers.

I mean, when I was back in High School, it was obvious

which teachers cared about their students and which ones didn't.  A

lot of it would just be regurgitation of facts and expecting the

student to retain the facts enough to be able to muddle up some

passing grade.

I didn't want to do that.  Instead, I wanted my students to create a 3-page essay on what sort of insights they'd gained in the class.  I wanted to see what they'd actually thought of and learned.

I was pleasantly surprised at a lot of the answers.  A couple of the guys, and I know who they are, simply wrote very large to try and fulfill the requirements.  At least they were creative, so they didn't get F's.

I had quite a few actually express how they never really thought of English literature as important in any way, not until I taught them how we're all impacted by it, whether we know it or not.  One even talked about an old movie he'd seen, where our stories continue on.  I'm pretty sure I know what movie he's talking about.

Some said I'd changed their lives, that they were looking at others with a lot more compassion.  I had one guy tell me that he thought it was a shame that I'd no longer be "Ms. Thurber" next year, but "Mrs. Mills." He said he had a crush on me since the first day.  It was flattering, and his statement was bold.

But, today, Molly officially left High School, and, of course, our parents flew out for it. I mean, it was kind of a familiar spectacle, a lot of students in caps and gowns, Molly, of course, being the Valedictorian, standing up there and giving some kind of speech, but that wasn't the biggest surprise.

Sure, Dad and Martha flew out. First to support Molly and, second, to help with the wedding preparations. When Dad and Ryan met, I saw a bit of machismo going on there as Dad told him about winning the heart of his "little girl." Ryan didn't challenge him or anything. I mean, he knows that, for the longest time, it's been Dad and me, before Martha came into our lives.

Ryan took me under one arm, held me close and promised Dad that he'd never hurt me, that he'd do everything he could to ensure I'd be very happy. Dad nodded, accepting that, then shook his hand before telling him he had some things to pass on to him later.

Martha just blushed, but then the big surprise happened.

Ryan took us all out to eat, and then they surprised us big time. Dad announced that he and Martha were very happy their family was growing, and not just from the inclusion of Ryan in it.

Martha's face glowed at that, and Dad asked her if it would be okay

if he broke the news.

After she nodded, her eyes shining, he asked both Molly and

me if we thought it'd be okay if we also had another one in the

mix…a baby brother.

### *Martha's pregnant!*

She's about 3 months along, but, once that news came, it was

so obvious to see.  We all jumped up, hugging her and Dad,

congratulating them.

And they already know my baby brother's name.  It'll be

Benjamin Nield Thurber Junior, or BJ for short.

Now, not only are Molly and I sisters, but we have a baby

brother too!  That is so exciting!


July 4, 2028

I can't begin to tell you what a relief and a blessing it's been

to have Martha-mom and Dad here to help plan this wedding.  I

mean, sure, Dad's being the doting husband and everything, making sure Martha-mom has whatever she needs or even craves.  I've heard of him even going out, middle of the night, for pickles.

I know that pregnancy can bring on some strange cravings, but at least Martha-mom, as I now call her, hasn't had anything really strange.  Still, it's barely out of her first trimester.

And Molly can't stop rubbing Martha-mom's tummy.  I mean she just can't stop herself.  It's like she's trying to connect to our baby brother, and, I'll admit it, I can't stop myself either.

For a good portion of my life, I've been an only child.  Sure, I know Mom and Dad tried, a lot, to give me a younger sibling, and it's what I kept praying for.

And then, a few years after Mom died, he met Martha, a widow with a teenaged girl, and the two of them fell in love.  It seemed like such a miracle when they finally got married, sealed together, and invited Molly to be sealed with them.

Which means I got myself a little sister.  And now, a baby brother.

Dad commented, the other day, that BJ would probably have a similar life to what he did, having nieces and nephews around his age.  I know what he was suggesting, but I'm not sure just yet when I want to have children of my own.  Ryan and I haven't really discussed it, but he's the patient kind of man, so I'm sure he'll agree.

Doesn't mean we won't be doing a lot of what makes children.  He's heard the rumors about redheads in the bedroom and wondered if he was ready for that kind of a thrill ride.  I had to tell him it was probably just a rumor, but he knows how agile I am.  We'll just have to see.

But then, today is the 4th of July.  America's birthday.  I know that, for a while, a few people who were mostly concerned with promoting racism tried to say that America really began in 1699, but that can't be further from the truth.  At the time, America was still a British territory, and, yes, I know that slavery was legal then, but slavery is more than just darker-skinned people and lighter-skinned people.

Slavery is when any person has domination over any other group of people, demanding to have something from them, some kind of work, in order to provide as meager a living to them as they can so that they stay dependent on their "master." And, yes, slavery has been illegal in America for a very long time, but it still goes on.

I can't tell you how much it pains me to know that there are girls and young women, many of them my age, who sell that best part of themselves in order to please a "master." How many others are there that show the private parts of themselves or display acts of lewdness in order to please a list of clienteles who, in all likelihood, would never care about them in the slightest? Of course, I'm talking about prostitution and virtual prostitution, aka pornography.

Yes, those girls and young women are slaves. It's no wonder many who think they're just making money end up strung out on drugs or alcohol, wasted away, because they don't let these people who use and abuse them see their real selves, the wonderful people they can be.

So, no, America did begin in 1776 with the proclamation that *everyone* has the right to life, liberty, and the pursuit of happiness. Sure, it took a while for us to realize that it really did mean *everyone*, but we're still getting there.

And yet there are so many who try to deny that is the right of every person.  They want us to forget that these rights are integrated with the laws that say that everyone has them.  Instead, they want us to hate not only others but ourselves as well, and for what?  Hatred can't be sustained for long; it has to continuously be stoked.  I've seen people try to stoke that, too.

No, love is the real key here.  It's so easy to give, so easy to receive.  When we can acknowledge that we're not all the same, that there are those who might have different skin colors, different eye colors or different hair colors, and see them all as children of our Heavenly Father, we gain knowledge, and we learn.

But here I am, pontificating again.  I guess Dad's right, that when we get wisdom, we need to make sure we understand it fully.

And I didn't even talk about the best part of what today brought.  Sara and Ethan showed up here to help with the last two weeks of this wedding, and I swear I could see Sara from a mile away because she was *positively glowing.*

And no wonder, the girl is obviously pregnant.  I mean, she's definitely got a pretty good-sized bump going on.

It was when we were all together that Sara had her arm in Ethan's and already announced that they were going to name the boy after his father.  His name would be *Benjamin.*

Martha-mom turned and glowered at Dad who swore he never touched Sara, but Sara burst out laughing as I looked, trying to understand what was going on.  She put her arm around me and told me she could never play that kind of joke on me.  She informed me that the boy's *middle name* was Ethan, and that was the name she meant.

And then she had an even bigger surprise when she told me the *girl's name would be* <u>*Aurelia Martha*</u>.

Yes, my best friend is having twins, and she named them after four of her very best friends.  She told Molly that she'd have to name another girl after her, name the second girl Molly Faye, which had Sara's kid sister grinning.

I mean, my whole family's here, ready to celebrate the formation of *MY FAMILY!*

And we're growing, although Sara couldn't help but say that I needed to catch up fast, winking in the process.

July 17, 2028

I'd say that I woke up this morning knowing that, tonight, everything would be different, but that would kind of be only a half-truth. I didn't sleep at all last night. I mean, everything was already set up, everything just perfect, but I knew that everything would be different later.

Molly and Faye helped me into the dress that I'd be wearing most of the day, a modest, lacy dress which Faye designed to accent my waist and hips. Sara and Martha-mom tried to get my hair and makeup done, although Sara did admit that I never did need much makeup. Still, they wanted everything to be perfect. I wanted everything to be perfect.

Yes, it's my birthday. I'm 24 today, but I'm getting the best birthday present I can, a husband. That's why everything is so different today. Martha-mom has her birthday as well, and she's all sorts of emotions. Partially from her pregnancy, I'm sure.

We got to the Ogden Temple about 10 in the morning. Dad, of course, thought everyone looked positively lovely, but was amazed at how his little girl had grown up to be a magnificent woman.  He's one of the witnesses today.

Ryan and I had to go and get the official document signed by Dad and Father Mills, our two witnesses, to make it all official and everything except for the actual ceremony.  Then Ryan was led to the men's locker room, and I was ushered into the bridal chamber. Martha-mom and Sara were both there, ready to get me out of this dress and into the ceremonial robes.  It felt so surreal, knowing that I was in there as the bride.  It felt kind of like I was saying goodbye to myself.

I'd never used the side entrance into the Celestial Room to go into the room, but there was Ryan, waiting for me, with a huge grin on his face.  He has such kind eyes and a welcoming smile.  He makes me feel safe.

We sat, just holding hands, just wanting to be together.  I looked around, marveling again that the elegance, the majesty of this room.  How many people had passed through here, doing what we're about to do?  How many passed through, having their own endowments done?  How many passed through doing endowments

for others?

But, this time, I swore I could feel something more.  I mean,

first time I came into a Celestial Room, I saw Mom.  This time,

though, I could feel her nearby.  I knew she was there, watching out

for us and approving.

I had to wonder, though.  I mean, I've seen a few temples in

my time, and all of them are majestic, as if they really are God's

houses.  And I've seen, maybe, three Celestial Rooms, all of them so

elegant, so perfectly clean and spiritual.

All too quick, or maybe it wasn't, the Matriarch came and

told us it was time.  Time to make this man mine for all Eternity.

Sure, there are divorces in the Church of Jesus Christ of Latter-Day

Saints.  Sometimes marriages that are done in the temples just don't

work out.  Sometimes an outside force influences them to break this

covenant.

I wasn't worried about that at that moment.  All I knew was

that I had to keep walking as Ryan held my hand.

The Sealing Room seemed so much larger than before, like there were hundreds watching.  All our ancestors and all our descendants were likely there to see this, I had a feeling.  I looked over at the far end of the room to see Dad just smiling and nodding.

I mean, I could go on about how marriage is supposed to be Eternal here.  I could go on about how important it is for our progress, both physically and spiritually.  I could go on about how the mirrors on opposite ends reflect into eternity.

But all I could think about as I knelt across the altar from Ryan and took his hand was how I felt at the moment.  I mean, over the past few years, I've been in love.  I've had times when I felt my heart break.  I've had times I felt so ordinary, but I've always had someone watching out for me, keeping me up.  That was important.

And now here was Ryan.  Here he was, promising that I'd be his one and only forever.  That he'd be with me no matter what. That he'd be my one and only.

And I promised the same.  We were to experience everything together.

And Dad was at the end.  Did he know how much he'd taught me?  Ryan reminded me so much of him, his gentleness, his character, his humor.  He'd never hit me, never even raised his voice except to get over my voice.  I never felt like I wasn't loved, wasn't cared about.  I never felt alone.

Sure, Dad did have to discipline me once in a while.  He'd always said that discipline came first, then being a rule-setter, then a friend.  He was, and still is, my best friend, and that won't change because of today.

It seemed like forever and only a few minutes before the sealer pronounced us husband and wife.  I'd done it.  I'd finally done it.  I'd gotten married.

Ryan reached across the altar, gently caressing my face before gently pulling me to him.  As our lips touched, a thousand fireworks went off, and I felt myself melting.  I wanted, so badly, to be able to just take him there, but it wasn't time yet.

As we stood, the sealer announced that, although it wasn't actually an important part, it was still traditional for the bride and groom to exchange rings.  Ryan pulled out this elegant platinum band, gently placing it on my finger, then winking at me and telling me I'm stuck with him.  I had to laugh and tell him I had the better end of that bargain.

We went back to change into our other clothes, now as a married couple.  It still seems so glorious to think of that.  Here we are, now, a married couple.  Married.

As we finally got back together just inside the Temple entrance, Ryan kissed me again, calling me "wife." In return, I called hm "husband."

We left the Temple amidst a crowd of well-wishers and onlookers who cheered like we were some kinds of celebrities. Honestly, I felt like one, like it was perfect.

We had a quick lunch, Dad joking that, if Aunt Anna were there, she'd likely say we were marred.  I had to laugh at the inside joke.  She called Mom and Dad that, although she was, like, very young at the time.  She's always been a lot of fun to hang around, but now, it was someone else's turn.

It was only an hour before the reception, so Ryan and I just barely had time to get things settled.  We'd take care of the rest later, I knew.  I felt excited, nervous, sick to my stomach and aroused at the fact that, in a short time, I'd no longer be the Redhead Virgin, which name they gave me so long ago when I went to High School.

But we went back to the Stake Center, all decked out.  I'd chosen Sara as my Maid of Honor, along with Molly and Faye.  Faye'd gone above and beyond, trying to make her big sister's dress to emphasize the fact that Sara was expecting twins.  As I hugged them all, I kept a hand on Ryan's arm.  It seemed so surreal, so out-of-this-world.

And then the other surprise fell when we were in the greeting line.  Sure, everyone was bringing gifts.  I mean, that's part of the whole thing.  Sara had thrown a great Bridal Shower, hinting that she'd probably insist on a Nursery theme, but it was kitchen related.  And, it seemed, so were the gifts.

It had been about an hour after greeting everyone in line.  Okay, probably not an hour, but my leg was starting to ache.  I leaned on Ryan a little, trying to get some support, when Sara got that strange smile on her face, one of recognition. I had to look over to see who's just come it.

Scott Hawkins walked in with a beautiful woman I'd never met and a little girl. I caught my breath, but Ryan noticed. I didn't think I had time to explain exactly who Scott was before his wife reached us first.

She practically gushed over me, telling me that all Scott could talk about for the first couple of months after they met was this gorgeous girl who was on her mission. She'd been so jealous of me, wanting to know everything about me. I had to laugh, not out of any guilt or anything but because I could acknowledge I'd been jealous of her as well.

I have to admit, I had no idea what I'd feel when I saw Scott again. I mean, I'm married to Ryan now, and that's a done deal, but I felt that same fluttering as before, like it was all fresh and new, even though I know it wasn't.

Scott hugged me, telling me he always thought I'd make a beautiful bride, and he was right. I had to thank him before he introduced me to his daughter, *his daughter Aurelia*. He named his oldest after me, as if I was someone worth remembering.

And maybe that's exactly what it should be, a pleasant memory, something that felt so good that it stays with me. Yes, we're both married to different people now, but we'll always have that memory of the time we shared.

I'm totally in love with Ryan, but I don't think I'll ever really stop loving Scott. But Ryan has nothing to worry about because that's not how I love Scott anymore. Yes, that'll always be there, but it's a memory.

But then the line kept going.

After what seemed like forever, I was able to sit as the dancing began. My bouquet was beautiful, no doubt, but it was time for food and for dancing. I still had my sweet tooth, so there was also a bowl of candies at every table.

Then the time came for our first dance as husband and wife. We'd chosen the song "I Want to Grow Old With You" from the move "Up." And I did want to grow old with Ryan. I so wanted to grow old with him. That was now in the running.

Then Dad got up and sang the song "I Loved Her First." I couldn't tell you the emotions that came over me when he actually used ASL to sing it directly to me, knowing ASL since my days as a High School student. I'd used it only occasionally, but he learned all the words as he sang along.

Then he got down and the song he chose for us came on. "My Little Girl" from Tim McGraw. He had tears in his eyes as we danced, no real rhythm. He told me something that I hadn't ever thought of before.

Ever since I'd been born, he'd known how precious I am. That's the meaning of my name, more precious than gold. He knew I'd need guidance and that I'd need someone to support me in everything. He knew I'd be someone really special as I grew up.

And he knew that, one day, he'd have to fully let me go. He knew that it'd be that day when I met a man I wanted to call my husband, and that day was today. Sure, I'd always be his little girl. I told him that, but I'm fully a woman now, and he told me that. He told me how proud he is of me, that I grew beyond his expectations, and I chose a man to call my husband who would grow to meet the pure angel I have become.

He kissed my cheek, telling me he loved me as the song ended, and he let me go to my husband.  I guess I was in tears too, because Ryan asked if I was okay.

I just told him I'd be just fine.  It was something very touching Dad told me.

Well, to put the long story short, Molly caught the bouquet. Ryan tried to be funny getting the garter off, trying to lift my dress up to show my legs and everything, but he knew better.  His Best Man caught that, and Molly let him slide the garter on her leg.

Then there was more, but Martha-mom and Sara tracked me down.  They wanted a private word with me, asking me if Dad had asked to speak to Ryan alone.  I remembered that a couple of days ago, he had.  Martha-mom gave Sara a knowing look and a huge smile that meant something before.  Sara just laughed a little good-naturedly, but in a knowing way before she told me what the whole thing was really all about.

Apparently, Dad had told Ethan, when he and Sara got married, the secret to *making love to a woman.* He'd passed on some things that he'd learned, knowing that it would really give Sara the ultimate pleasure in the act.

*And, apparently, it worked.* Martha-mom grinned, saying that she also knew how that secret felt, knowing that every time she and Dad made love, she'd always felt so intense, so great, so much like she was the only woman in the world for him.

They both nodded, telling me I was about to know it.

I don't remember too much about cutting the cake afterwards, except that I smashed the piece in Ryan's face after he did in mine. I was nervous, beyond nervous, knowing what Dad told Ryan.

And here it is, now, 3:00 AM. I guess it's the 18th now, and I'm so beyond thrilled, beyond happy.

I mean, I've never been able to appreciate how wonderful it is to be touched. I've never so *felt good in my skin.* I've never felt more loved, more beautiful, than what happened a few hours ago when Ryan made love to me for the first time.

Sure, I know that people have sex all the time, but it's so much more vital, so much richer, when you know that the person who you're making love with has committed to you, and to you alone, that you're the only one they want to experience this with. It's so much better, knowing that the commitment is there.

He made me feel so alive, more alive than ever before, as we consummated this union.  My heart is still racing, my skin still tingling at the memory of that touching and caressing.

I guess I'm no longer Ms. Thurber anymore.  I'm Mrs. Mills.

And we'll have to see what the future holds.


January 18, 2039

Man, I can't believe I nearly forgot about these diaries.  I mean, yeah, I've kept more from the time I got married, but, in reading these, I can see all the ways I may have made mistakes and may have grown up to the point where I was ready to be married.

It's in my other diaries where I wrote about the wonders of having a life growing inside me, about two years after we got married.  That was RJ, my little rapscallion.  When his Uncle BJ is here, the two of them are inseparable.  I mean, the wonders, the

anxieties, the thrills and the moodiness are all in there, as was the

pain of that first birth and the incredible joy afterwards.

Then there was Amanda Grace, the one I had two years

afterwards.  Named for my mom, she inherited her kindness and her

gentleness.  She's the apple of her daddy's eye, that's for sure.

Then there's Betty Ruth, named for my Paternal

Grandmother, and the one to carry on the redheaded gene.  That girl

is curious about everything, even though she's only 3 now.  I can't

tell you the number of times I've had to go and rescue her from

some inherent danger that she may have put herself in.  But we love

her nonetheless, and she's always had a handout for us.

There is a new one on the way, another boy.  The same thrill

and joy is there, having that little life growing inside me.  I mean,

I've heard all their heartbeats when they were inside me.  I know

they were all alive, sure, living off of me solely, but they were ours.

Yes, Ryan and I are still married.  Sure, we've had

arguments.  We've had out and out fights even.  But we always

remember what Dad told us, that, even though we're a couple, we're still two different individuals.  We'll have differing ideas, different

takes.  Sometimes we may rub each other the wrong way, but

patience and prayer and knowing that the other person has a right to

be heard as well can put an end to it.

Ryan is now head coach at the High School, but most of his

time is spent here, at the ranch.  When his parents passed away, we

got the big house, and our kids took over the place with gusto.  I'm

Vice Principal at the school, and most of the students think I'm

tough, but I'm fair.  I mean, I don't take any guff from anyone about

anything, but, if someone has a problem and they need to talk to

someone about it, my door is usually open.  Most of the time, it's the

staff that talks to me, but that's okay.

Sara and Ethan moved here a few years ago, and they now

have *five children*.  Yes, Molly Faye was their second girl, and then

another set of twins.  She's now *Head Nurse* at the hospital here,

and everyone thinks she does a great job.  Nobody has complained

about the nursing staff since she took over.  Ethan is doing his

contracting work, which means more homes for Ogden.

Molly is in Provo, with her husband and two kids.  Yes, I'm still Aunt Aurelia, and they learned to say my name right the first time.

And then there's Dad and Mom.  I don't remember when I started just calling Martha "Mom," but it's been a while.  Today is Dad's 65th birthday, and his age is showing.  Mom is always by his side, and he tried to keep up with BJ and Roxie.

Oh yes, I forget to mention that they had a little girl a couple of years after BJ was born, Roxanna Grace.  She is headstrong, wanting to get her way in everything, and hates being contradicted, but she's also one of the kindest children I know.

BJ, of course, loves being an uncle and loves hanging out with us.  He usually hangs on every word I say, which is kind of cute in its own way.

But, today, we moved Dad and Mom here.  Dad, of course, grumbled the whole way, but I think he's secretly delighted he gets to spend time with his grandchildren.  I know they love him because of that glow he always has.  He's always been so good with kids.

But we moved him here, Mom insisting that we can take care of him better here.  She's going to be school nurse at the school, knowing someone in the administration can pull the strings for her.

Anyway, we built a house for them, ground level, so that the children can have their own rooms, which really excited Roxie.  Dad and I have stayed close through the years.  I mean, that feeling didn't end when I got married, but he's still my best friend.  Now he's a 2-minute drive away instead of a phone call, and I can look in on him whenever I want.

So, my life has had its ups and downs.  I'm still diabetic, which hasn't passed on to any of my children yet, and I still get treated for depression and anxiety, but I can't really complain about anything.  My family is all around me, which is fantastic.

Sure, I'm only 34, but I feel like everything is the way that it should be, like someone designed it to be like this, so good, so excellent.  Mom and Dad are always willing to help when they can, which may be a lot more now that they're not so far away.

So, I guess that just about wraps everything up.

<u>*The End*</u>

*For my good friends*

*Talon David and Chelsea Napier*

*Thank you so much for putting up*

*With the ramblings of a madman*

*Who wanted to tell the story of a daughter*

*That doesn't exist.*

*Hopefully we can work together some more*